The Blue Mountains

USING THIS BOOK

One of the best ways of helping children to read, is by reading stories to them and with them.

*The first time you read this book, read the **whole** story to the child, looking at the illustrations together. Then, if the child is reading confidently, give him* the book to read on his own, whenever he wishes. If you think that more help is needed read the story again with him on another occasion, reading the left-hand pages yourself and asking him to read the right-hand pages. Build up his confidence by praise and encouragement as much as you can.*

*The child is referred to as 'he' in order to avoid the clumsy 'he or she', but the book is equally appropriate for girls and boys.

British Library Cataloguing in Publication Data
McCullagh, Sheila K.
 A dragon in the mountains. —(Puddle Lane reading programme. Stage 5; v. 2)
 1. Readers—1950-
 I. Title   II. Davis, Jon   III. Series
 428.6   PE1119
 ISBN 0-7214-1027-8

First edition

Published by Ladybird Books Ltd Loughborough Leicestershire UK
Ladybird Books Inc Lewiston Maine 04240 USA

Printed in England

A dragon in the mountains

written by SHEILA McCULLAGH
illustrated by JON DAVIS

This book belongs to:

Ladybird Books

The clock in the Magician's room
struck twelve.
The Magician put down his book.
"I wonder what happened to the boy
who used to strike the hours,"
he said to himself. "There was
a girl, too. They both went
to the magical Country of Zorn.
I wonder what happened to them."

The Magician took a silver bowl
of magic water from a shelf,
and looked down into it.
The water changed to greeny-blue,
and then it became
as clear as glass.
It was like a window,
looking into the Country of Zorn.

The Magician saw a boy and girl
on the grass by a blue lake.
"I remember their names, now,"
he said to himself. "Irun and Sandella.
I'm glad they are safe,
in the Country of Zorn."
The water in the bowl changed to blue.
When it cleared again,
the Magician saw a new picture.

A fire dragon was making its way
up a rocky path in the mountains.
As the Magician watched, a flame
of fire shot out of its mouth.
A bush burst into flames.

The Magician pushed back his chair.
"The City of Zorn is in danger!" he cried.
"If that fire dragon reaches the city,
no one will be safe!"
He thought for a moment.
Then he went to a cupboard.
He took out a little red bag,
and a jar of silver seeds.
He poured a handful of seeds into the bag.
Then he went to the window, and
gave a long, low call.

A great white swan
came flying in through the window.
She landed on the Magician's chair.
"What do you want, Magician?"
asked the swan.

"I want you to fly to the
Country of Zorn," said the Magician.
"A fire dragon is making its way
through the mountains, towards the city.
A boy and a girl live there.
They are called Irun and Sandella.
Give this bag of silver seeds to them.
Tell them that they must plant the seeds
between the cliffs, across the mountain path.
The seeds will grow in the moonlight.
They will grow into trees in one night.
No fire dragon can pass a silver tree.
If he touches it, he will turn into stone.
But only Irun or Sandella must touch
the silver seeds of the silver trees.
If anyone else in the City of Zorn
touches them, they will turn into stone, too."

The Magician hung the red bag
around the swan's neck.
"Fly, swan, fly!" he cried.
The swan opened her wings, and
flew out of the window,
over the trees and across the hills
towards the Country of Zorn.

Irun and Sandella were by the lake with
Alanna, when the swan flew down and
landed on the water in front of them.
"Are you Sandella? Are you Irun?"
cried the swan.
"Yes," they both answered.
"I have a message for you
from the Magician," cried the swan.
And she told them what
the Magician had said.
"A fire dragon!" cried Alanna.
"I must warn the people of Zorn."
"There is not much time," said the swan.
"I saw the fire dragon on the path,
as I flew over the mountains."
"We must go at once," said Sandella.
"If the fire dragon is coming,
there is no time to be lost."

"Aren't you afraid?" asked Alanna.

"Yes," said Sandella. "But we must go."

"I'm afraid, too," said Irun. "But
no one else in Zorn can touch
the seeds of the silver tree.
We must go."

Sandella lifted the bag of silver seeds
from the swan's neck.
"Where is the path?" she asked.
"The path runs through that wood,"
said Alanna, pointing to some trees.
"It runs right up the mountain
to the cliffs. You can't miss the way.
It's the only path."
"I will fly on ahead of you,"
said the swan. "I will meet you
at the cliffs, on the mountain."

She spread her wings, and
flew over the wood, and on
up into the mountains.

Alanna had a bag of food with her,
which they had been going to eat
by the lake. She gave it to Irun,
and the two children set out at once
towards the wood, while Alanna
ran back to the City of Zorn,
to warn the people that
a fire dragon was in the mountains.

As soon as Irun and Sandella
came to the trees,
they saw the path, and
ran along it.

When they came to the end of the wood,
they saw that the path led on,
up the mountain side.
It was steep and rocky, but
there was only one path, and
they scrambled up it as fast as they could.

Higher and higher they went, until
at last they saw the Valley of Zorn
spread out like a map below them.
The sun was beginning to set
behind the mountain tops,
and the rocks and cliffs above them
changed from grey to red.

The sun had gone, and the light
was fading from the sky, when at last
Irun and Sandella came to the pass
through the mountains.
There were high cliffs on each side,
and a patch of grass between them.
A little stream fell over the rocks
in a white waterfall.

The swan was standing on a rock
by the stream.
"Plant the seeds here,
in a line between the cliffs,"
she called.
"Plant them before the moon rises,
so that they can grow tonight,
in the moonlight."

Irun and Sandella each picked up
a sharp stone.
Sandella opened the little red bag,
and set it on the ground.
They each took a handful of silver seeds
from the bag.

Sandella went to the foot
of the cliff on the left, and Irun
went to the cliff on the right.
They began to plant the seeds
in a long line across the path.

The ground was very hard.
Sandella was so tired, that her hands
shook a little, as she made the holes
with a sharp stone.

Irun was longing to rest too, but
he knew that they mustn't stop now.
There wasn't much time.

"Drop a silver seed in each hole,"
cried the swan. "Don't cover the seeds.
Let the moon shine on them.
They will grow in the moonlight."

Irun and Sandella moved slowly across the ground between the cliffs, planting the silver seeds.

Sometimes they stumbled, and fell.
But they got up again, and went on.

Irun had just planted the last seed,
when there was a cry from the path.
They looked across, and saw
a strange little animal standing there.
It was something like a squirrel,
and something like a cat,
and it was a blue-green in colour.
"What's that?" cried Irun.
"It is one of the quorns,
who live in the rocks," said the swan.
"What is it, Quorn? Tell us,"
called Sandella.
"We come from the City of Zorn.
We are planting the silver trees."

"You're too late!" cried the quorn.
"The fire dragon is coming.
The fire dragon is coming up the path
from the Dark Valley."

At that moment,
the moon rose over the mountains,
and fingers of moonlight touched
the holes where the seeds were planted.

There was a sudden flame by the rocks
on the far side of the pass,
and they saw a fire dragon crawl
over the rocks, breathing out flames
as he pulled himself along.

"We must stop him!" cried Irun.
"We must stop him, until the seeds
have time to grow."
"This way," cried the quorn. "Quickly!
Come this way, and throw rocks
down on his head."
The little quorn ran to the cliff,
and began to climb up it.

Irun and Sandella followed him,
but the cliff was steep, and
their hands were shaking.
Somehow, they managed to pull themselves
up onto a great rock,
which jutted out over the path.

There was a pile of loose rocks there,
which had fallen down from the cliff.
"Quick!" cried the quorn. "Quick!"
The fire dragon was almost below them.
Irun and Sandella picked up the rocks,
and hurled them down
on the fire dragon's head.

The fire dragon looked up and saw them.
A long flame shot up towards them.
The fire dragon tried to climb the cliff,
but the cliff was too steep.
They were just out of reach.

"Help me with this," cried Irun,
pushing a big rock, which lay
on the edge, just above the fire dragon.

Sandella flung herself at the rock,
and they pushed as hard as they could.

The rock crashed down
on the fire dragon's head,
knocking the dragon back
to the foot of the cliff.
For a moment, it lay quite still
on the ground.

"Quick!" cried the quorn. "Quick!
Climb back to the path.
The silver trees are growing."

Sandella looked across to the grass.
A row of little silver trees stood across
from one cliff to the other.
They were only as tall as Sandella,
but as she looked, she could see
that they were getting taller.
Their leaves shone and sparkled
and danced in the moonlight.
They were the loveliest trees
Sandella had ever seen.

"Quick!" cried the quorn. "Quick!"
Sandella and Irun scrambled
down the cliff after the quorn,
as the fire dragon shook its head
and began to move again.

41

By the time the fire dragon
was back on the path,
Irun and Sandella were safe
on the far side of the trees.

They saw the fire dragon lift itself up,
and gaze at the line of silver trees.
It gave a last roar of rage,
turned round, and started back
the way it had come.

"I shall leave you now," cried the swan,
flying over their heads.
"You are safe now, behind the silver trees.
I must fly back to the Magician."
"Thank him for us," cried Irun.
"I will," called the swan.

She flew up high into the air.
Irun and Sandella watched
until she was out of sight.
Then they looked for the quorn,
but the quorn had gone.

"I'm too tired to go back
to the city tonight," said Sandella.
"So am I," said Irun. "But it's cold
up here on the mountain.
We must try to go down."
They heard a cry from below them.

They looked, and saw the people of Zorn
coming up the path towards them.
Alanna was calling to them,
and waving a lantern.
"We shall be safe now," said Irun,
and together they walked slowly
towards Alanna, and the people of Zorn.

If you have enjoyed this longer story, here is another one for you to read:

Stage 5
1 **The Magician's raindrops**
This is about the time when Sarah and Davy ask the Magician to help them to protect the mice who live in his garden.

The Magician, Davy and Sarah

Hickory Mouse and his friends

Tom Cat comes into the garden to catch
the mice who live in the hollow tree. When
Sarah and Davy ask the Magician to help,
he decides to make some magic raindrops
to stop Tom Cat – but some other strange
things happen as well.

Tom Cat

There are five stories which tell you how Irun and Sandella came from Candletown to the Country of Zorn.

Stage 4

1 When the clock struck thirteen

tells you how the iron boy came to the Country of Zorn.

2 The sandalwood girl

is the story of what happened to a girl, carved out of wood, who was in the attic of the old house when the clock struck thirteen.

The story of the iron boy continues in

3 On the way to the Blue Mountains

which tells you about the adventures of the iron boy and the sandalwood girl, as they go on their dangerous journey.

4 The fire in the grass

continues their adventures.

5 The Silver River

tells of how the children are carried to the Blue Mountains by the silver ponies. When the boy and girl have bathed in the river, they become like ordinary children and finally meet someone who tells them their names.